This book belongs to . . .

For my dad, Michael Sharratt,
and snowy days shared together

PUFFIN BOOKS

UK | USA | Canada | Ireland | Australia
India | New Zealand | South Africa

Puffin Books is part of the Penguin Random House group of companies
whose addresses can be found at global.penguinrandomhouse.com.

www.penguin.co.uk
www.puffin.co.uk
www.ladybird.co.uk

Penguin
Random House
UK

First published 2021

001

Text and illustration copyright © Nick Sharratt, 2021

The moral right of the author has been asserted

Printed and bound in China

The authorized representative in the EEA is Penguin Random House Ireland,
Morrison Chambers, 32 Nassau Street, Dublin D02 YH68

A CIP catalogue record for this book is available from the British Library

ISBN: 978-0-241-51911-0

All correspondence to:
Puffin Books, Penguin Random House Children's
One Embassy Gardens, 8 Viaduct Gardens, London SW11 7BW

MIX
Paper from
responsible sources
FSC
www.fsc.org   FSC® C018179

Oh No! Shark in the Snow!

Nick Sharratt

PUFFIN

On a cold day in winter
a dad and his son
take a walk in the park
for some afternoon fun.

Timothy Pope, Timothy Pope
has brought along his telescope.

As snowflakes tumble in the air,

he looks left,

he looks right,

he looks everywhere.

And this is what he sees.

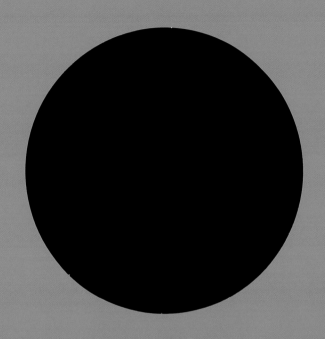

It's a bit of a shock.

Young Tim whispers, "Oh no!"
Then he takes a deep breath
and yells,

"SHARK IN THE SNOW!"

A shark? Tee-hee-hee!
That's the top of a tree!

Timothy Pope, Timothy Pope
looks again through his telescope.

As snowflakes fall without a sound,

he looks left,

he looks right,

he looks all around.

And this is what he sees.

That strange shape is back.
Tim's *quite* sure this time, so
in the blink of an eye he shouts,

"SHARK IN THE SNOW!"

Well, look at that.

It's a girl in a hat!

Timothy Pope, Timothy Pope
has another look through his telescope.

As snowflakes float
and spin and glide,

he looks left,   he looks right,

he looks far and wide.

And this is what he sees.

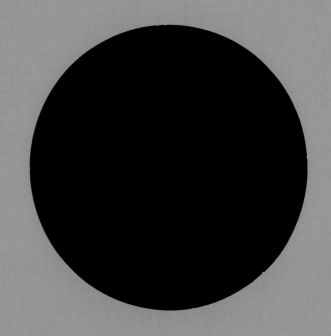

Tim trembles all over.
The next thing you know –
he's roaring out loud and clear,

"SHARK IN THE SNOW!"

A shark?
No, wait . . .

It's the tip of a skate!

The lake's frozen over.
It's covered in ice
and someone is merrily skating.
How nice!

Timothy Pope, Timothy Pope
keeps looking through his telescope.

He doesn't look left,
he doesn't look right.

He stands still as a statue
to take in the sight.

Because this is what he sees.

Tim's eyes get wider,
his mouth makes an "O".

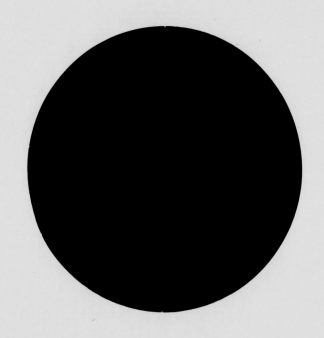

He's spotted . . .

"AN ICE-SKATING SHARK IN THE SNOW!"

It's not a shark –
it's Santa
in his suit of
red and white!

He's getting in
some exercise
ahead of his
big night.

He sees them and skates over.
"Hello, Dad, and hello, Tim!
Now, have you both been good this year?"
"Oh yes!" they say to him.

"I know you have," laughs Santa,
"and I've got some gifts for you."
From his sack he takes two parcels.
Tim's is green and Dad's is blue.

"Don't open them till Christmas Day!"
adds Santa with a smile.
They thank him for their presents
and they chat with him awhile.

Then Santa says, "I've got to dash –
there are reindeer to be fed.
Goodbye, my friends!" And in a flash! . .

. . . he's just a speck of red.

A dad and his son
head back home, cheeks aglow,
and completely forget
about sharks in the snow!